LEGO® CITY

FIGHT THIS FIRE!

By Michael Anthony Steele
Illustrated by Chuck Primeau

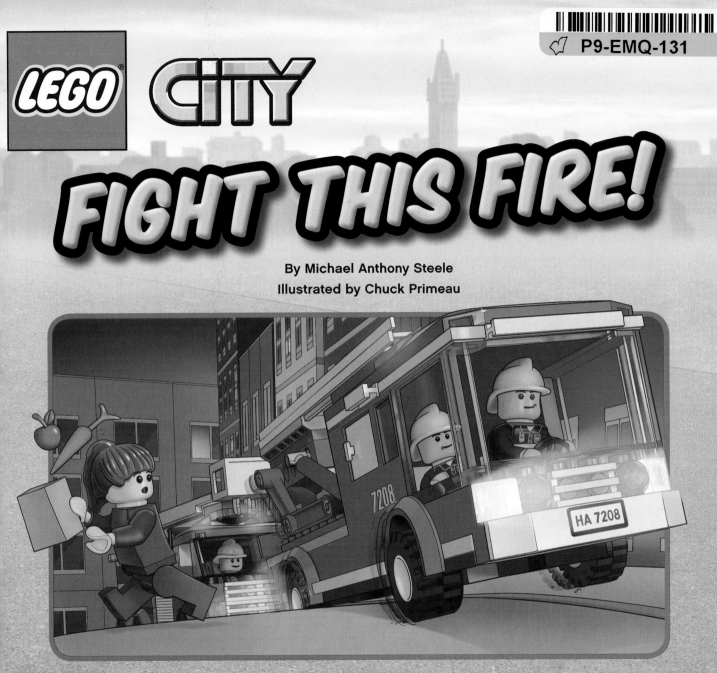

SCHOLASTIC INC.

NEW YORK   TORONTO   LONDON   AUCKLAND

SYDNEY   MEXICO CITY   NEW DELHI   HONG KONG

ISBN 978-0-545-31759-7

LEGO, the LEGO logo, the Brick and the Knob configurations and the Minifigure are trademarks of the LEGO Group. ©2011 The LEGO Group. Produced by Scholastic Inc. under license from the LEGO Group.

28 27 26   19 20/0

Printed in the U.S.A.   40
This edition first printing, August 2011

"Good morning, Rookie," said the fire chief. "Welcome to the LEGO® City Fire Department!"

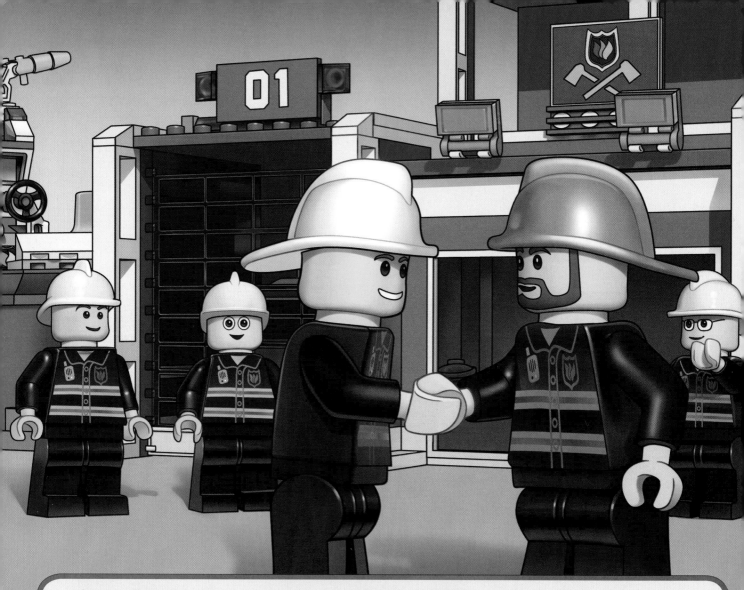

The chief met the rookie in front of the LEGO® City fire station. Other firefighters were there to greet him.

"Let's see what you learned at the Fire Academy," said the chief. "We have to find out what kind of firefighter you'll be."

"Water is a firefighter's best friend," said the chief.

A firefighter named Splash handed the rookie a fire hose. "Be careful," said Splash. "These hoses can get away from you."

"Thanks," said the rookie. He aimed the hose and twisted the nozzle.

"*Whooooooah!*" The powerful stream of water blasted the rookie into the air.

Down below, the chief and firefighters ran for cover. Splash darted to the fire truck. He quickly turned off the water valve.

The rookie was safely on the ground again. The chief and the other firefighters were dripping wet.

The chief marched up to the rookie. "You'll have to work on that," he said. "Let's try something else."

"Sometimes we have to fight fires at sea." The chief pointed to a few flaming barrels floating in the water. "Do you think you can put out those barrel fires?"

"Yes, sir," answered the rookie.

"Good," said the chief. "Floater will take me out in the motorboat to watch."

The rookie climbed aboard and got behind the water cannon.

"How do you aim this thing?!" asked the rookie. "Look out!" The water from the cannon shot right past the floating barrels. It blasted the tiny motorboat instead. The chief and Floater fell into the ocean.

"Sorry about that, " said the rookie.

"That's fine," replied the chief. "There are plenty of other jobs we firefighters do. Maybe you'd be better working with the helicopter crew."

"Yes, sir," said the rookie.

This time, the chief decided to watch from a safer distance. He was tired of getting wet.

He spoke into his radio. "Good job, Rookie," he said. "Now dump the water onto the burning building. You have to time it just right."

The rookie didn't dump the water in time. He missed the burning building and hit the helipad instead. The water splashed all over the chief. "Not again!" shouted the chief.

"Sorry again, sir," said the rookie.

"There must be something you're good at." The chief sighed and shook his head. "We'll figure it out tomorrow. Go down to the rec room and get some sleep."

Later that night, the fire alarm sounded. *BRRRRRIIIIING!*
The chief nearly fell out of his chair. "Let's go, firefighters!" he shouted. "We have a real fire to fight!"

A firefighter named Spanner ran up to the chief. "Gears is still out sick," Spanner reported. "He can't drive the main fire truck."

"I can do that," said the rookie. Before the chief could say anything, the rookie jumped behind the wheel and started the engine.

WEEEEOOOOOOEEEEEEEEE!
The siren howled as the fire truck sped down the road. The rookie controlled the big truck with ease. He safely turned corners and swerved through the heavy traffic. The young rookie was a natural behind the wheel!

The rookie pulled up to see a tall apartment building on fire. Thanks to his driving, they had arrived before the fire grew too large.

While the other firefighters fought the fire with hoses, the rookie raised the tall ladder and helped trapped people escape the flames.

"Thank you very much," said one of the residents.

"Great job, Rookie," said the chief. "It looks as if you'll be a LEGO® City firefighter after all."

"Thanks, Chief," said the rookie.

"Now, since you're so good with that fire truck . . . " The chief chuckled. ". . . take it back to the station and give it a good washing."

"Yes, sir," said the rookie.

The chief smiled at him. "Just let me know before you start. I don't want to be around when you turn on the water hose."